a minedition book
published by Penguin Young Readers Group

Copyright © 2006 by John Rowe
Coproduction with Michael Neugebauer Publishing Ltd. Hong Kong
Published simultaneously in Canada.
Manufactured in Hong Kong by Wide World Ltd.
Designed by Michael Neugebauer
Typesetting in Frutiger by Adrian Frutiger
Library of Congress Cataloging-in-Publication Data available upon request.
Color separation by Fotoreproduzioni Grafiche, Verona, Italy.

ISBN 0-698-40043-7
10 9 8 7 6 5 4 3 2 1
First Impression

For more information please visit our website: www.minedition.com

J. A. Teddy

by John A. Rowe

minedition

Once upon a time there was a fearless Pirate called Captain Scallywag, who lived at number 14 Smith Street with his Mom and Dad.

Everyday, he and his friends sailed off around the world in their little boat, in search of adventure. And everywhere he went his trusty bear J.A. Teddy was at his side.

But one day, they were attacked by pirates, and Teddy fell overboard and was lost.

Captain Scallywag searched everywhere, but he couldn't find him.
Poor Teddy was lost, perhaps for ever and ever. Big teardrops rolled
down Captain Scallywag's cheeks.

Nearby, some pixies were busy hanging their laundry out to dry when they heard Captain Scallywag's sobbing. "What on earth can the matter be?" they asked him.

"I've lost my Teddy," sobbed Captain Scallywag, and then he cried even louder. This made the pixies cry too, for they hate to see someone so upset.

Before long some goblins and elves came to see what all the fuss was about. When they heard about poor Teddy, they, too, began to cry. Just then, the Queen of Fairies passed by, and when she heard what had happened she told Captain Scallywag about a castle in a faraway land, where all teddy bears go when lost by children.

"But it's far, far away," she warned, "and the door is locked and guarded by a giant ogre!" Captain Scallywag dried his tears and turned slowly to his brave shipmates, each one as fearless and courageous as a lion.

"Men!" he said, "We must rescue the teddy bears!"

And as night fell, many more little people came to help the brave sailors. They banged drums and blew tiny trumpets, while fairies fanned a gentle breeze with their wings and filled the little boat's sail with fairy dust.

Soon it began to float gently upwards into the warm night sky. And fireflies guided the ship through the darkness.

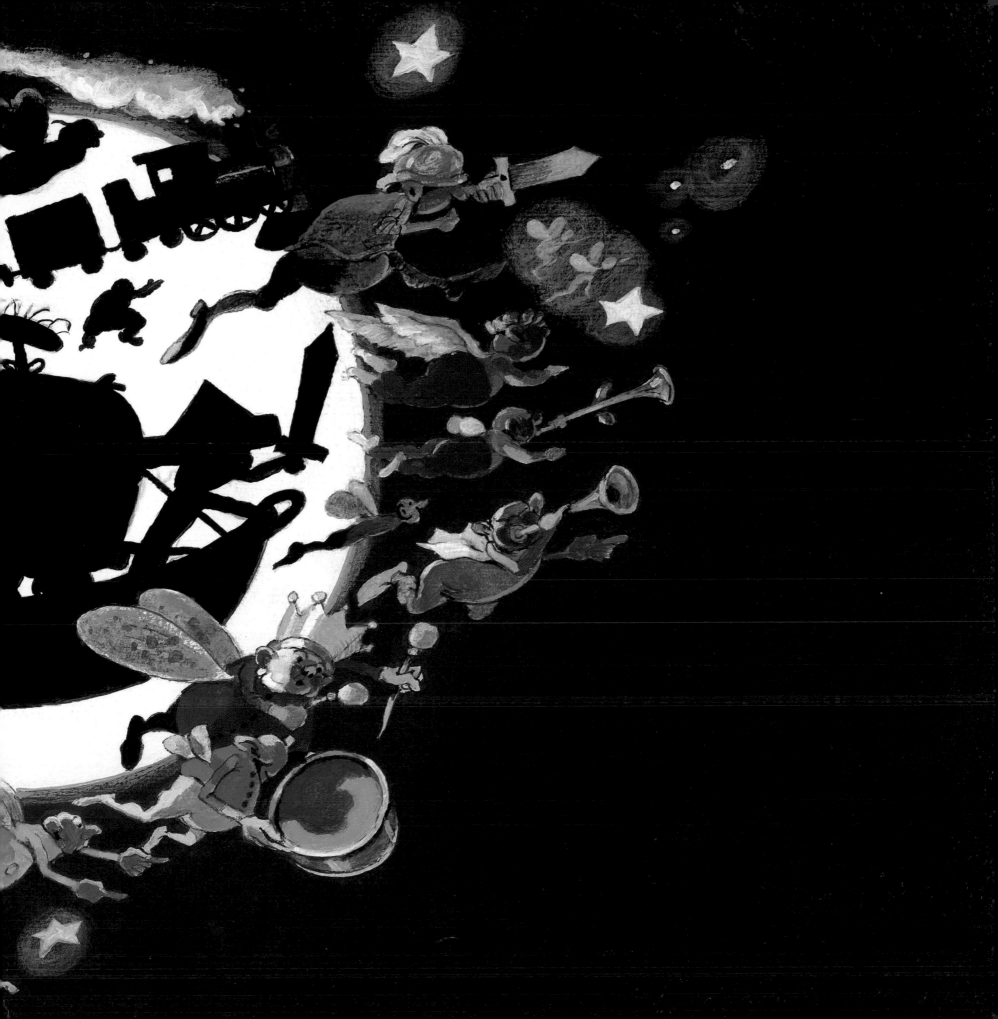

Suddenly, Captain Scallywag called, "Land ahoy!" and threw the anchor overboard. Far below stood the castle, and guarding the door was the giant ogre . . . sleeping like a baby.

Very quietly the little people crept up on him, and before he knew what was happening, they jumped all over him! They pulled his ears and tickled him while they found the key to the door. "What's going on?" he cried. "Get off!" But it was too late.

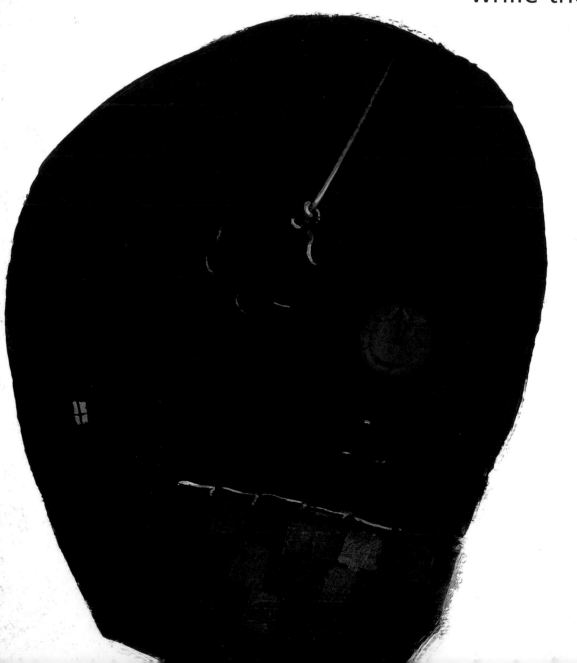

Captain Scallywag rushed toward the door and unlocked it.
In the darkness of the room were hundreds of teddy bears, dusty and
unloved. They huddled together for comfort, a ticket tied to each
bear's leg. And on each ticket was written the ghastly word
"LOST."

The bears rubbed their eyes and smiled at Captain Scallywag.
Then, very slowly, they moved toward the open door and began
walking out into the night. And suddenly, an amazing thing
happened. They all began to float upwards! Up and up they went,
higher and higher, into the moonlit sky.
Soon, hundreds of bears began to fly away into the darkness, their
"LOST" tickets flapping behind them.

But where was Teddy? Captain Scallywag couldn't find him anywhere. Soon all the bears were gone except for one very dusty one, hiding frightened in the corner. Could it be? "Teddy," whispered Captain Scallywag, "Is it you?"

The little bear turned his head and suddenly ran towards him.
"Oh Teddy!" cried Captain Scallywag,
"It really is you!
I will never, EVER,
lose you again,
I promise!"
He gave Teddy a big,
BIG hug.

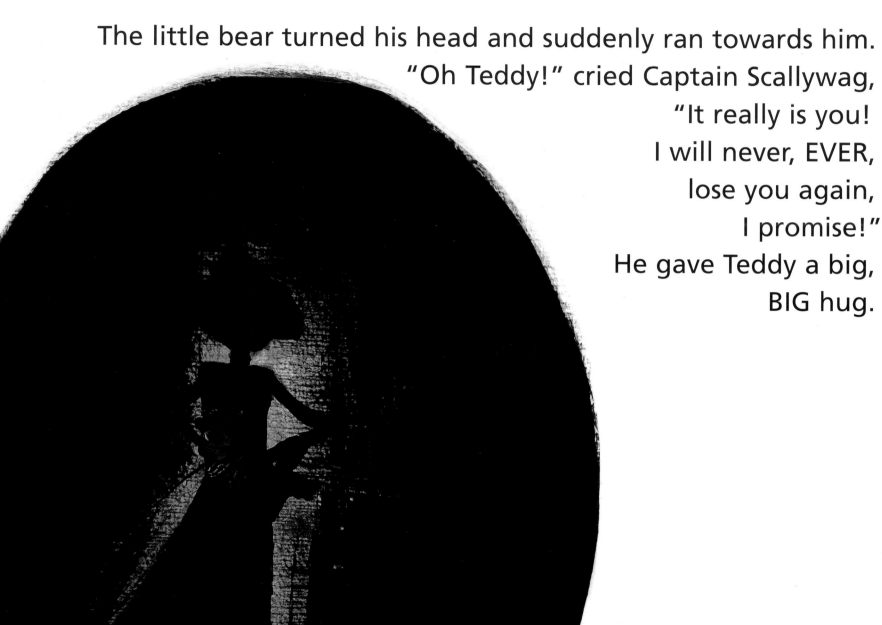

Now Captain Scallywag suddenly felt very, very tired, and he laid down in the warm grass for a moment's rest. He closed his eyes. And no sooner than he had, he heard his Mom's friendly voice calling to him. "Time for dinner!"

As he ate, Captain Scallywag told his Mom excitedly all about the fairies and the pixies and the goblins and the elves and the pirates. But she just laughed and hugged him. "You fell asleep in the garden my brave little pirate, and you've been dreaming again!" she explained. "I think it's time you were in bed."

And Captain Scallywag laughed too. Soon he was tucked up safe and warm in bed with Teddy by his side. But later that night, as he reached out to give Teddy a hug, he felt something strange. Tied around Teddy's leg was a piece of string with a small ticket attached. He could just make out the word that was written on it . . .

"Oh Teddy," whispered Captain Scallywag, "it wasn't a dream after all! I did rescue you from that ogre!"

And the very next morning, all over the world, there were cries of delight and happiness as children everywhere awoke to discover their lost teddy bears snuggling happily up against them, once again safe, and where they belonged.

All thanks to the kindness of a few special little people and one very brave pirate.

Afterword

The giant ogre appeared on TV and in all the newspapers. He told everyone that he had seen fairies and pixies and elves and goblins led by a fearless pirate captain, but nobody believed him. Well, would you?